MRS. PEACHTREE
and the Eighth Avenue Cat

Erica Silverman
illustrated by Ellen Beier

Macmillan Publishing Company   New York
Maxwell Macmillan Canada   Toronto
Maxwell Macmillan International   New York   Oxford   Singapore   Sydney

Library of Congress Cataloging-in-Publication Data
Silverman, Erica. Mrs. Peachtree and the Eighth Avenue cat / Erica Silverman ;
illustrated by Ellen Beier. — 1st ed.   p.   cm. Summary: In turn-of-the-century New York, a stray cat appears at
Mrs. Peachtree's Eighth Avenue tea shop and becomes attached to the owner, despite her best attempts to resist it.
ISBN 0-02-782684-8 [1. Cats—Fiction.] I. Beier, Ellen, ill. II. Title.
PZ7.S58625Mr 1994   [E]—dc20   92-16973

10939

To Lil Moed, in memory — E.S.

To M., M., S., and especially P. — E.B.

The cat pressed his nose to the window of Mrs. Peachtree's Eighth Avenue tea shop. His coat was scruffy, and the corner of his left ear was bitten off.

"Must that cat stare like a fool in love?" said Mrs. Peachtree.

"Maybe he's hungry," suggested a customer.

"So? Do I look like a fish cake?"

That evening, alone in her flat above the store, Mrs. Peachtree watched the lamplighter making his rounds. Later, in the flickering glow of the gas lamp, she saw the cat's shadow.

"I suppose I could feed him just this once." She cut up a bit of chicken and took it downstairs.

The cat purred. He circled her skirt.

"Don't you try to butter me up, cat," she said.

The next day, Mrs. Peachtree was stacking tins of tea. The postman opened the door. "I didn't know you had a cat," he said.

"I don't," replied Mrs. Peachtree.

Up jumped the cat. Tins toppled everywhere.

"*Mrow*," said the cat.

"*Mrow*, yourself," said Mrs. Peachtree. And she chased him out. "Scat, cat! And don't come back!"

At closing time, Mrs. Peachtree walked up Eighth Avenue to deliver a basketful of tea.

"Hey, lady!" a wagon driver shouted. "Your cat's about to get trampled."

Mrs. Peachtree looked back. "Fool cat." She picked him up. The cat purred.

At the corner, she put him down. "Now go away. You are not my shadow," she said. "And I am not your fish cake."

While she was eating dinner, Mrs. Peachtree glanced out her window. The cat stared back. "I can't just let him starve." She cut up a bit of meat pie and took it downstairs.

The cat ran in.

"Who invited you, cat?" She pushed him out. Then she lingered on the stoop, watching him eat.

Early in the morning, Mrs. Peachtree heard the milkman's wagon coming down the street. *Clip-clop* went his horse. *Clinka clinka* went the milk bottles. *Clinka clinka...crash!*

Mrs. Peachtree hurried outside. She glared at the cat.

"*Mrow,*" said the cat.

"*Mrow,* yourself." She chased him away. "Scat, cat! And don't come back!"

Day after day, the cat sat on the stoop. Customers stopped to pet him.

"You have a nice cat," said a man.

"He's not my cat," said Mrs. Peachtree.

One evening, Mrs. Peachtree leaned out the window.

"*Mrooowwww!*" howled the cat.

"You again?" grumbled Mrs. Peachtree. She cut up a bit of herring and took it downstairs.

The cat ate. Then he rolled over.

"You can't bamboozle me with your cute tricks," she said. Then she sat beside him, watching the carriages roll by.

A few days later, the iceman brought
a block of ice for Mrs. Peachtree's icebox.
In came the cat. He dropped something at
Mrs. Peachtree's feet.

"What a good mouser," said the iceman.
"He's brought you a present."

"He'll scare off my customers!" cried
Mrs. Peachtree. She grabbed her broom.

The cat squinted up at her.

"But he likes you," said the iceman.

"He thinks I'm a fish cake," said Mrs. Peachtree. She swept the cat out the door. She swept him off the stairs. She swept him down the street. "Scat, cat! And don't come back!"

The iceman climbed into his wagon. "Smells like rain," he said.

Mrs. Peachtree looked up. Dark clouds were moving swiftly across the gray sky.

All afternoon, Mrs. Peachtree listened to rain beating on the glass.

A customer came in. "Where's your cat?"

"I don't have a cat." She glanced out at the wet stoop. "What do you suppose cats do in the rain, anyway?"

"They get cold and wet and scared," said the customer.

"Oh, dear," said Mrs. Peachtree.

Gusts of wind rattled the windows that night. Lightning flashed across the sky. Mrs. Peachtree stared down at the deserted street. "Fool cat must be out there somewhere."

She cut up a bit of liver. She put on her raincoat and went downstairs.

"Here, cat. Time for supper, cat." She searched the alley.

"Lose something?" asked the lamplighter.

"Just a cat," replied Mrs. Peachtree. "Have you seen him?"

"No one should be out on a night like this," said the lamplighter. "Not even a cat."

Mrs. Peachtree shuddered.

In the middle of the night, she got up. She gazed out the window for a long time.

By morning, the rain had stopped. Mrs. Peachtree hurried downstairs. She stared at the untouched plate of food.

Then she went next door to the hat shop. "Have you seen a cat?" she asked.

"The scruffy thing that sits on your stoop?" said the milliner.

"He's not that scruffy," said Mrs. Peachtree. "Have you seen him?"

"No," said the milliner.

Mrs. Peachtree walked up and down Eighth Avenue. She peeked into window boxes. She peered under wagons. She poked behind stairways.

"Have you seen a cat with half a left ear?" she asked the greengrocer.

The greengrocer shook his head. "But cats are like that," he said. "They come and they go."

"Oh," said Mrs. Peachtree. She trudged home.

"Where's your cat?" asked the milkman.

"I don't have a cat." Mrs. Peachtree sighed. "Not anymore."

In the shop, she cleared off the counter. Slowly, she scooped tea leaves into tins.

The postman opened the door.

Mrs. Peachtree turned. "Have you seen—"

Up jumped the cat. Tea leaves scattered everywhere.

"Look at that!" said Mrs. Peachtree. "My cat came back!"

The cat purred.

Mrs. Peachtree laughed. "Call me fish cake," she said. "And I'll call you Shadow."

"Mrow," said Shadow.